DAUGHTER OF EARTH

A ROMAN MYTH

RETOLD AND ILLUSTRATED BY

Gerald McDermott

DELACORTE PRESS / NEW YORK

Imagine a time, long ago, when the world was divided into three kingdoms.

Above, among the clouds, Jupiter, the king of the sky, ruled the heavens.

Below, beneath the ground, Pluto, king of the dead, ruled the Underworld.

Between the heavens and the Underworld ruled the goddess Ceres and her beautiful daughter, Proserpina.

They tended the hills and the fields. The meadows blossomed with flowers, and the wheat grew thick and tall.

Ceres and Proserpina made the earth green the whole year round, for in that time, long ago, the year had no seasons.

The people on earth lived in awe of Jupiter, and they were afraid of Pluto. But they loved Ceres and Proserpina for their bountiful gifts of life. They did not know that all this would soon change.

Pluto's underworld kingdom rested on the body of a sleeping giant. Ages before, the giant had been buried under a mountain of rock and had slept ever since. But from time to time he shifted beneath his burden. When he did, the ground broke open, steam shot up through the cracks, and Pluto's palace threatened to topple.

At these times Pluto would harness his horses and race his golden chariot through the passageways of the Underworld, searching for fallen pillars and crumbling walls. It was on such a day that his steeds pulled him toward the surface of the earth....

On that day the goddess Ceres was walking over the earth. As always, wherever her robe touched, wheat sprang from the ground, and wherever her feet touched, flowers blossomed. At her side ran Proserpina, filled with happiness at the beauty of the hills and the fields.

When Ceres had finished her work, she turned to Proserpina and said, "I must visit the other gods, but I won't be gone long. Don't wander away alone. Stay here and play with Cyane. You'll be safe, my darling, by the edge of the pool."

Proserpina waved as her mother flew into the sky. Then she looked at the fields thick with flowers and laughed in delight.

"I'll make a bouquet," she called to her friend Cyane, a water nymph, "and surprise Mother when she returns."

Before Cyane could stop her, Proserpina dashed into the fields. She filled her arms with poppies and hyacinths, with crocuses and iris. Soon she had strayed far from the pool. She was about to turn back, her arms overflowing with blossoms, when she saw a narcissus, a flower more beautiful than any she had ever seen.

She ran to pluck it to add to her bouquet. She grasped the stem and began to pull. But the stem did not break. She pulled harder. The ground shuddered. Once more she tugged. The earth groaned. Then she heard a crack.

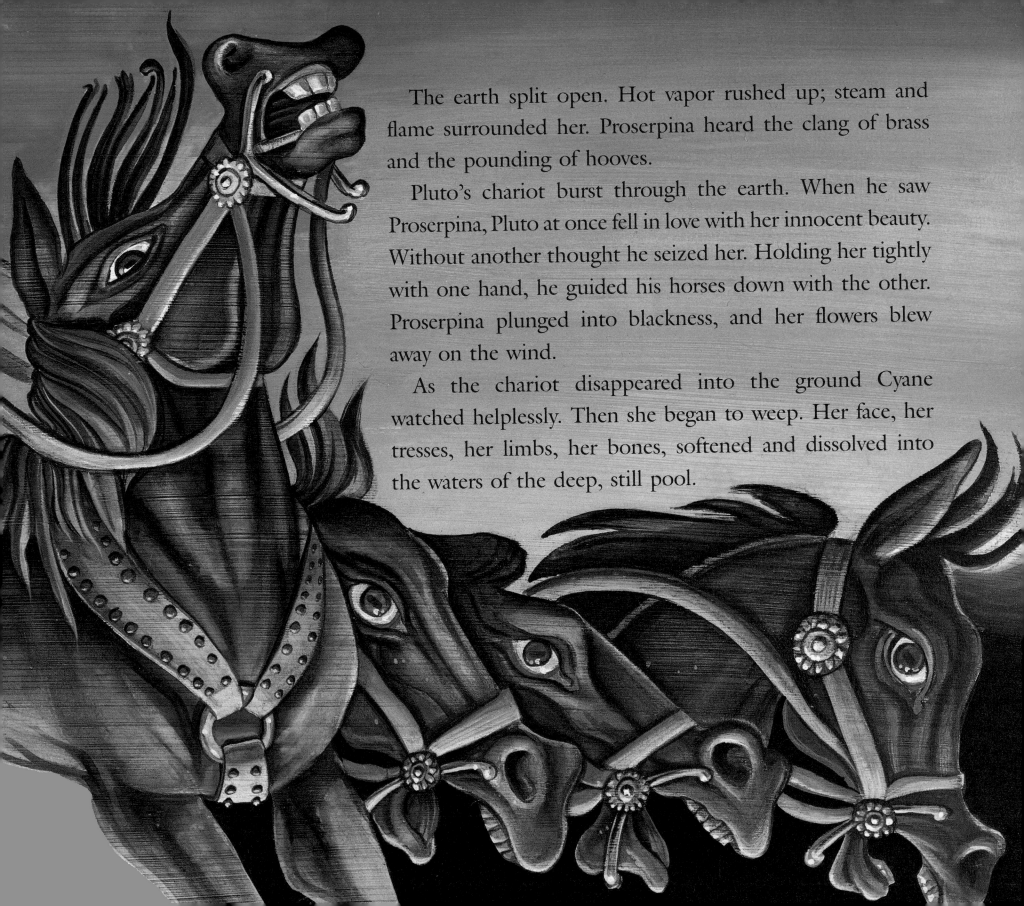

The earth split open. Hot vapor rushed up; steam and flame surrounded her. Proserpina heard the clang of brass and the pounding of hooves.

Pluto's chariot burst through the earth. When he saw Proserpina, Pluto at once fell in love with her innocent beauty. Without another thought he seized her. Holding her tightly with one hand, he guided his horses down with the other. Proserpina plunged into blackness, and her flowers blew away on the wind.

As the chariot disappeared into the ground Cyane watched helplessly. Then she began to weep. Her face, her tresses, her limbs, her bones, softened and dissolved into the waters of the deep, still pool.

Pluto's horses bolted down the corridors of the Underworld. Proserpina struggled to free herself, but Pluto clutched her more tightly.

"Don't be afraid," he said. "You will be my bride and my queen."

Pluto and Proserpina forded the Styx, the river of eternal sleep. Along the shore Proserpina saw the souls of the dead wandering in the darkness, and she became even more frightened.

"Mother, help me!" she cried. "I will not stay here."

"No one can hear you now," Pluto said as they drew to a halt at the gates of his palace. Pluto led her into his gloomy home and seated her on a cold marble throne. There Cerberus, the three-headed hound who guarded the palace, kept watch over her. Proserpina grew as still as death.

High in the clouds Ceres had heard her daughter's cries.
She rushed to earth and ran across the fields. Only a few
broken blossoms were lying on the surface of the pool.

"Where is my daughter?" she cried.

Her weeping echoed through the valleys, and the flowers
in the fields began to die.

For long days Ceres searched for Proserpina. She traveled across fields of barley, through forests deep in shadow, and over mountaintops. The birds stopped singing as she passed; even the leaves on the trees turned brown and fell. Wherever she spilled her bitter tears the grass withered.

At last, after Ceres had searched the earth, she turned to the heavens.

"Jupiter, what has become of my daughter? Surely you must know."

Jupiter and the other gods looked down from the clouds. He had seen Pluto burst from the earth and carry Proserpina beneath the ground. Yet he knew he would offend Pluto if he interfered. He and the other gods said nothing.

Only Sol, the god of the sun, had pity on Ceres and spoke. "Your daughter is in the Underworld," he said.

Ceres gasped. "But only the dead go there!"

"She is not dead. Pluto has stolen her. He will make her his bride."

Ceres's face grew dark.

"His unwilling bride!" she cried. "O gods, you have betrayed me. You are cowards to turn away. Pluto may rule the Underworld," she said, "but I have power over the earth. Remember me when the crops no longer grow and the people are hungry. Then will I have my revenge."

All the while, deep below, Proserpina sat silently on her cold marble throne. Her skin had grown pale and her face was sad.

"Here you shall want for nothing," said Pluto. "Look around you. Jewels and precious stones—all yours if only you will be my bride. And there! Breads and meat for you to eat. Our wedding feast!"

Proserpina said nothing. She wanted no glistening jewels, only the bright sunlight. She wanted no bread or meat, only the sweet fruit of the green earth. She wanted no part of marriage to Pluto. In her misery she longed for the warmth of her mother's embrace.

"Why can't I make you happy?" Pluto sighed. Frowning, he sank onto his couch. If only he could entice her to eat of the food of the dead. Perhaps the ruby-jeweled pome-granate would tempt her. Then, by the laws of the Under-world, she would belong to him forever.

Meanwhile, Ceres kept her word.

"I will give no more until my daughter returns," she said. Wrapping her cloak tightly about her, she withdrew into a cave.

As Ceres mourned Proserpina's absence the earth mourned with her. The birds no longer sang. Nothing grew. The people began to go hungry. With each day that passed the world became more barren.

The gods looked down and saw the toll their silence had taken. The world was joyless and cold.

Shivering in despair, the people called out to the gods for food. The gods saw that they must act. And so Jupiter dispatched fleet-footed Mercury to bear a message to Pluto. Down to the depths Mercury sped, through the corridors of the Underworld, to pound at the gates of Pluto's palace.

"You must release Proserpina at once," the messenger of the gods called out, "so that she may return to her mother."

Stubborn, his voice filled with anger, Pluto roared from the palace.

"No! She will be my bride and dwell with me forever."

"Pluto, listen well," said Mercury. "You have wrongly taken her, and you may not keep her here against her will. She is of the living. Has she eaten of the food of the dead? If not, you must let her go. Jupiter commands it."

Pluto scowled and thought for a moment. "I dare not refuse the king of the gods," he said at last.

He opened the gates and allowed Mercury to enter.

"Give me but a moment," whispered Pluto. "Let me speak with her alone before she departs."

As they walked down the passageway Pluto said to himself, "I will tell her I have decided to let her visit her mother. Perhaps she will have kind thoughts of me and want to return someday."

He went into the chamber and stopped in surprise. The hungry Proserpina had found a fresh pomegranate, which he had left for her, and was tasting its bittersweet juice.

Pluto gasped. "You're eating!" he cried. Then he broke into laughter. "You are mine forever," Pluto said. "You have eaten of the food of the dead." He shouted to Mercury, "She *must* remain with me." His voice rang with triumph.

"O gods," Proserpina cried out. "This is not just. I ate but three small seeds!"

Mercury flew away, his heart breaking.

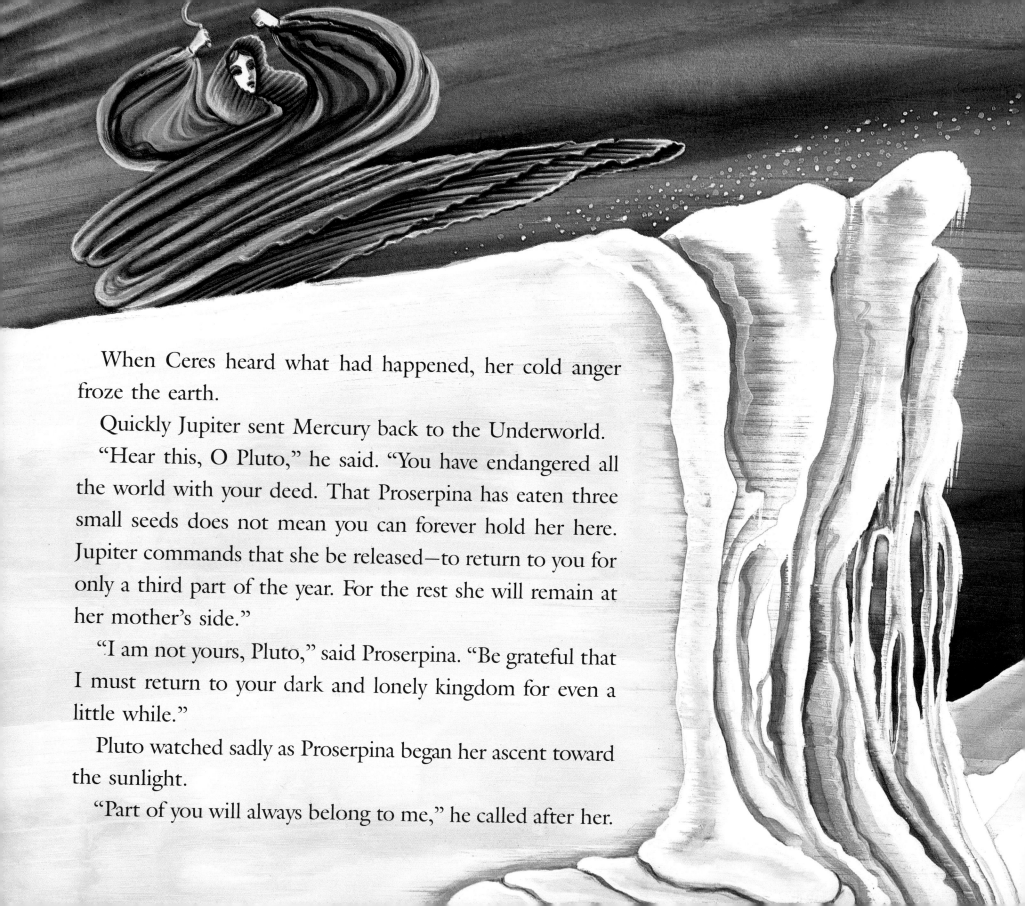

When Ceres heard what had happened, her cold anger froze the earth.

Quickly Jupiter sent Mercury back to the Underworld.

"Hear this, O Pluto," he said. "You have endangered all the world with your deed. That Proserpina has eaten three small seeds does not mean you can forever hold her here. Jupiter commands that she be released—to return to you for only a third part of the year. For the rest she will remain at her mother's side."

"I am not yours, Pluto," said Proserpina. "Be grateful that I must return to your dark and lonely kingdom for even a little while."

Pluto watched sadly as Proserpina began her ascent toward the sunlight.

"Part of you will always belong to me," he called after her.

So to this day, once a year, Proserpina descends into Pluto's gloomy realm to sit silently by his side.

On earth this is the season of cold and darkness, and all growing things await her return.

Then, when she rises from the ground in glory, the birds sing in welcome, and the wheat and the grass and all the flowering plants begin to grow. Once more life begins, and the world is filled with the joy of spring.

Author's Note

Stories about the abduction of the daughter of the Earth Mother by the king of the Underworld have been told throughout the Near East and Mediterranean Europe for thousands of years. The tales were linked, in popular belief, to the passage of the seasons and the springtime renewal of earth's bounties. In ancient Greece and Rome this passionate drama was the basis of rituals of spiritual rebirth.

My retelling of the mother's search for her kidnapped daughter is based on the turbulent version in Ovid's *Metamorphoses*. Ceres (*SEE-reez*), the Roman goddess of vegetation, and her daughter, Proserpina (*pro-SUR-pee-na*), correspond to Demeter and Persephone of Greek mythology. The mother represents the ripened grain and the maiden the seed that lies buried within the earth, awaiting release. Their conflict with the other gods contrasts the fertile, nurturing, life-giving ways of the mother goddess with the patriarchal Olympian order—rigid and remote, imposing its rule from above.

In the myths of classical antiquity the River Styx (*STIX*) had to be crossed on the journey to the Underworld, where the gates were guarded by the three-headed dog, Cerberus (*SUR-ber-us*). The pomegranate symbolized love and fertility.

About the Author and Illustrator

Gerald McDermott is an artist whose illustrated books and animated films have brought him numerous awards and international recognition. His *Anansi the Spider,* an African tale, was a Caldecott Honor Book, and *Arrow to the Sun,* a Pueblo myth, won the Caldecott Award.

Born in Detroit, Mr. McDermott studied and worked in New York and France and now lives in Connecticut.

About This Book

The text type used in *Daughter of Earth* is Galliard, and the display typeface is Augustea Inline.

The book was designed by Jane Byers Bierhorst.

The artwork was rendered in gouache on illustration board prepared with gesso and was camera-separated.

Published by Delacorte Press
1 Dag Hammarskjold Plaza
New York, N.Y. 10017

FOR MARIANNA

Library of Congress Cataloging in Publication Data

McDermott, Gerald/Daughter of Earth.

Summary: When Pluto wrongly takes Proserpina to be his bride in the Underworld, Ceres, mother of Proserpina and goddess of the Earth, withdraws into a cave to mourn and refuses to permit crops to grow.
1. Ceres (Roman deity)—Juvenile literature.
2. Proserpina (Roman deity)—Juvenile literature.
[1. Ceres (Roman deity) 2. Proserpina (Roman deity) 3. Mythology, Roman] I. Title.
BL820.C5M37   1983   292'.13   82-23585
ISBN 0-385-29294-5

First printing

DATE DUE

MAY 01 2006	
MAR 17 2009	
	PRINTED IN U.S.A.

GAYLORD